To Mom and Dad,

You taught and demonstrated the self-sacrificing,

caring commitment that is Christ's unconditional love.

You put your love into action, and gave so many families the

hope and promise of Jesus through this most beautiful tradition.

This book is for you.

For Grant, Nixon, and Channing,

All that I am and all that I do is for you.

Thank you for blessing my life so abundantly.

This book is given with love

TO

_____

FROM

_____

SECRET SANTAS

And the Twelve Days of Christmas Giving

Written by **Courtney Petruzzelli** Illustrated by **Melissa B. Snyder**

You have been chosen by Santa himself,

to be a special kind of Christmas Elf.

You've heard of his list that he checks twice,

the one that shows him who's naughty and nice.

But did you know there's a secret one?
An exclusive list that's quite some fun!
A list that's full of girls and boys,
an elite group that Santa deploys.

He only chooses the kindest and best,

and to make his team, you must've impressed.

After watching your goodness all year through,

he has decided that his team needs YOU!

He's seen your kindness, compassion, and heart,

You've been perfect for this list from the start.

Sweet child, you've been given a marvelous gift,

the ability to make the world's spirit lift.

Santa needs your help to spread some cheer,

giving to someone who needs it this year.

The person you pick can be a neighbor or friend,

a teacher, a foster child, or war veteran.

For twelve days,

you'll leave a little surprise.

Wait 'til you see the joy fill their eyes.

Santa will leave instructions for prep,

and each night you'll drop a

gift at their step.

You'll run and hide so no one finds out,

it's YOU who's bringing this magic about!

Despite all their efforts to see who it was,

they'll only discover it's gifted with love.

You'll craft and create,
you'll wrap, and you'll bake.
It's so very exciting,
the difference you'll make!

Day one, day two, day three, day four,

a blanket, some gloves, and treats galore.

Day five, day six, day seven, day eight,

hot cocoa for sipping, and fudge on a plate.

Day nine, day ten, eleven, and twelve,

candy canes, ornaments, and Santa's sleigh bells.

He can't wait to watch all the fun to be had,

and see what love and blessings you'll add.

On the 1st Day of Christmas

It isn't about all the

gifts you receive,

it's what you can GIVE,

that's why people believe!

The joy and the hope

you'll spread this season,

that's what Christmas is for,

the real, true reason.

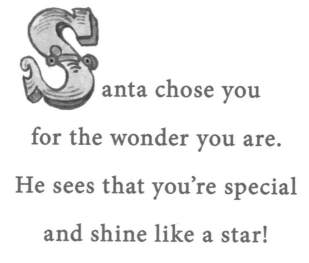

anta chose you
for the wonder you are.
He sees that you're special
and shine like a star!

Now that you're on
his exclusive team,
forever you'll stay there
and always be!
So, Secret Santa,
take up your mission,
and let's begin this
magic tradition!

OFFICIAL NORTH POLE CERTIFICATE

OF

Achievement

PROUDLY PRESENTED TO

_____

In recognition of your kindness, compassion, obedience and cheer,
You've gone above and beyond the nice list this year!
For showing the true spirit of Christmas,
Santa has deemed that you be awarded a spot on his

" SECRET SANTA TEAM "

Santa Claus

Santa Claus

Secret Santas:
A Christmas Tradition With Heart

Ask your family these questions to start your own Secret Santa tradition:

What does it mean to be part of The Secret Santa Team?

Who is someone in your life that is deserving or in need this Christmas?

What are some fun ways that you can do anonymous acts of kindness?

Why is it important to GIVE and not just receive during the Christmas season?

What is the true meaning of Christmas?

Share your story at
feedback@SecretSantaTeam.com

or via Social Media using the hashtag
#SecretSantaTeam

and find ideas for Secret Santa gifts on our Instagram
@secretsantateam

Claim Your FREE Gift!

 Visit:

PDICBooks.com/Gift

Thank you for purchasing

Secret Santas

and welcome to the Puppy Dogs & Ice Cream family.
We're certain you're going to love the little gift
we've prepared for you at the website above.

CPSIA information can be obtained
at www.ICGtesting.com
Printed in the USA
BVHW020357091122
651448BV00012B/958